ASTRID & APOLLO

AND THE
WONDERFUL WAX MUSEUM

BY
V.T. BIDANIA

ILLUSTRATED BY
CÉSAR SAMANIEGO

PICTURE WINDOW BOOKS
a capstone imprint

To the incredible students at Lakeshore Elementary School! –VTB

Published by Picture Window Books, an imprint of Capstone.
1710 Roe Crest Drive
North Mankato, Minnesota 56003
capstonepub.com

Library of Congress Cataloging-in-Publication Data
Names: Bidania, V. T., author. | Samaniego, César, 1975- illustrator. | Bidania, V. T. Astrid & Apollo (Series)
Title: Astrid and Apollo and the wonderful wax museum / by V.T. Bidania ; illustrated by César Samaniego.
Description: North Mankato, Minnesota : Picture Window Books, [2023] | Series: Astrid and Apollo | Audience: Ages 6 to 8 | Audience: Grades K-1 | Summary: The twins are participating in a class project to create a living "wax" museum, and they each have to choose a person whose statue they will pretend to be when the museum opens.
Identifiers: LCCN 2022048895 (print) | LCCN 2022048896 (ebook) | ISBN 9781484675458 (hardcover) | ISBN 9781484675410 (paperback) | ISBN 9781484675427 (pdf) | ISBN 9781484675441 (epub)
Subjects: LCSH: Hmong American children—Juvenile fiction. | Twins—Juvenile fiction. | Siblings—Juvenile fiction. | History—Study and teaching—Juvenile fiction. | Schools—Juvenile fiction. | CYAC: Hmong Americans—Fiction. | Twins—Fiction. | Siblings—Fiction. | History—Study and teaching—Fiction. | Schools—Fiction. | LCGFT: Novels.
Classification: LCC PZ7.1.B5333 Atk 2023 (print) | LCC PZ7.1.B5333 (ebook) | DDC 813.6 [E]—dc23/eng/20221114
LC record available at https://lccn.loc.gov/2022048895
LC ebook record available at https://lccn.loc.gov/2022048896

Designer: Tracy Davies

Design Elements: Shutterstock/Ingo Menhard, 60, Shutterstock/Yangxiong (Hmong pattern), 5 and throughout

Printed and bound in the USA. 5425

Table of Contents

Hi, I'm Astrid. My twin brother is Apollo, and we were born in Minnesota. We live here with our mom, dad, and little sister, Eliana.

ASTRID GAO NOU

Hi, I'm Apollo! Our mom and dad were both born in Laos. They came to the United States when they were very young and grew up here.

APOLLO NOU KOU

MOM, DAD, AND ELIANA GAO CHEE

gao (GOW)—girl; it is often placed in front of a girl's name. Hmong spelling: *nkauj*

Gao Chee (GOW chee)—shiny girl. Hmong spelling: *Nkauj Ci*

Gao Hlee (GOW lee)—moon girl. Hmong spelling: *Nkauj Hli*

Gao Nou (GOW new)—sun girl. Hmong spelling: *Nkauj Hnub*

Hmong (MONG)—a group of people who came to the U.S. from Laos. Many Hmong from Laos now live in Minnesota. Hmong spelling: *Hmoob*

Nia Thy (nee-YAH thy)—grandmother on the mother's side. Hmong spelling: *Niam Tais*

Nou Kou (NEW koo)—star. Hmong spelling: *Hnub Qub*

pa dow (PA dah-oh)—needlework made of shapes like flowers, triangles, and swirls. Hmong spelling: *paj ntaub*

tou (TOO)—boy or son; it is often placed in front of a boy's name. Hmong spelling: *tub*

CHAPTER 1

A Fun Project

"And that is what physics is about," said Mrs. Jackson just as the bell rang.

Science class was over. The students closed their books. Their science teacher opened the door to the hall.

"I'll see you all next time!" she said.

Astrid smiled. Today had been a great day in science class! Mrs. Jackson taught them a little about physics. She said it was the study of physical objects, from the smallest thing in the world to the whole entire universe.

The students took their science books and folders and walked back to their homeroom.

"Physics is so interesting!" Apollo said.

"I hope we talk about it more at the next science class!" Astrid said.

"Me too," Apollo said as they stepped into their classroom.

Mrs. Lor stood at the front board. She was waiting for the students to take their seats.

"Class, please get settled," she said. "We have a lot to discuss."

The students stopped chatting. They put away their supplies and looked up at the board, curious.

Mrs. Lor said, "I want to tell you about our language arts and history project. I promise it's going to be very fun!" Then she wrote on the board: *LIVING WAX MUSEUM.*

The class gasped in surprise.

Their teacher turned back to face them. "Have any of you heard of this before?" she asked.

The students shook their heads.

"A wax museum is a place where wax figures of famous people are on display for visitors to learn about. For this project, each of you will choose someone from history and research their life and their work. Then you will pretend to be a wax figure of that person for our museum," Mrs. Lor said.

Excitement buzzed through the classroom.

Mrs. Lor continued. "The day our wax museum opens, families and other students will visit our classroom. If someone comes up to you, your wax figure will come alive. You will be the person you researched and tell them about yourself."

Astrid and Apollo smiled. Mrs. Lor was right. This *would* be a fun project!

Mrs. Lor wrote on the board:

pick a historical figure

research their life

make a costume to dress as the person

practice telling facts about them

Astrid and Apollo's classmate Sabina raised her hand. Mrs. Lor called on her.

"Can we pick anyone?" Sabina asked.

"Please choose someone who made a special discovery or invention, who overcame challenges and did something remarkable. Someone who changed history," said Mrs. Lor.

Lily, Astrid and Apollo's cousin and classmate, raised her hand.

"You mean like Amelia Earhart, the first woman to fly a plane by herself across the Atlantic Ocean? People should know about her," Lily said.

"Amelia Earhart is a very good choice," said Mrs. Lor. "Yes, please pick someone you think we should learn more about. Pick someone that interests you too."

The students nodded.

"Here are examples of historical figures that students chose before. This may help give you ideas," said Mrs. Lor. "Gandhi, Martin Luther King, Jr., Cesar Chavez, Anne Frank, Ruby Bridges, Neil Armstrong . . ."

Astrid and Apollo's friend Kiran raised his hand and asked, "What about Ham the Astrochimp, the first chimpanzee who went to space?"

Mrs. Lor smiled. "You may research the person who thought of the *idea* for Ham to travel to space, but you can't choose Ham. No animals in the wax museum—only people!"

Kiran and all the students giggled.

CHAPTER 2

Something Important

The twins got off their school bus and raced home. They were excited to plan for the Wax Museum project.

"I know who I'm picking!" Apollo said.

"Already? Tell me!" said Astrid.

"I'll give you clues," said Apollo. He bent his elbows and put up both fists. Then he bounced from side to side.

Astrid grinned. "You're going to be Bruce Lee! The fists and bouncing gave it away!"

"You got it! I had to pick him. He's one of my heroes! What about you?" Apollo asked.

Astrid shook her head. "I haven't decided yet. But whoever it is, they're going to be amazing, like Bruce Lee!"

"I'll help you," Apollo said.

"Thanks!" Astrid said.

The twins opened their front door and walked into the house.

"Mom, we're home!" Apollo called.

"Hi kids! Be right there!" Mom said.

A trail of books standing up on their bottom edges lined the entryway.

Astrid tried to hop over the wall of books, but her shoelace caught on the corner of one book. She tripped and fell. The wall of books tumbled over with a thud!

"Ouch!" Astrid cried.

"Are you okay?" Apollo pulled her up.

Astrid rubbed her knees. She slid one of the books away from her foot. The cover showed an Asian woman wearing a white coat.

Mom came running toward them. "Gao Nou, are you all right?" she said.

Astrid nodded. "I'm okay."

Mom looked at the floor and sighed. "Eliana, come pick up your things!"

Astrid and Apollo's little sister Eliana hurried over from the living room. She was wearing a toy crown, and she carried a toy shield and a toy sword. Their dog Luna followed her, as always.

"Oh no!" Eliana said when she saw the mess of books. "My casso wall falled!"

"We'll help you build an even better castle wall," Apollo said.

Eliana smiled, and Luna barked.

* * *

After dinner, the twins went to the living room. Astrid curled up on the couch. Apollo sat on the rug by the coffee table.

He started looking through a stack of Dad's old sports magazines. He had found some that had pictures of Bruce Lee.

"Look! I want this as my costume for the wax museum." He pointed to a picture that showed Bruce Lee in a yellow jumpsuit. The bottom of the suit had long pants. The top had long sleeves. A black stripe ran down the sides of the jumpsuit.

"I've seen him wear that in posters!" said Astrid.

"It's one of his most famous outfits. He wore it in a movie and now everyone remembers him in it," Apollo explained.

"You'll look cool!" said Astrid.

"Thanks. I'll ask Mom to sew it for me. Now, let's decide who you should be," Apollo said.

Astrid shrugged. "I want someone brave who did something incredible."

Apollo closed the magazine. "I heard kids already picked George Washington Carver, Nelson Mandela, and Helen Keller," he said. "In class, Mrs. Lor talked about other famous people too. Did you like anyone from her list?"

"Well, they're all important," said Astrid. "But no one really stood out to me."

Their parents walked into the room.

"What if we ask Mom and Dad for help?" Apollo suggested.

"Good idea. They're the two most important people we know!" Astrid said, and the twins both chuckled.

CHAPTER 3

Know Their Name

Astrid turned to her parents. "Can you please help me with my Wax Museum project?"

Mom nodded. "That's the project where students study a historical figure and pretend to be that person. Is that right?"

Astrid and Apollo both said, "Yes!"

Dad smiled. "We'd love to help. Who are you thinking about?"

"Well, I want to pick someone amazing, but I don't know who.

Apollo already picked Bruce Lee," said Astrid.

Dad grinned and said, "Great choice." He put up both fists.

Apollo stood up and did the same. He and Dad bounced on their feet and pretended to fight each other with kung fu moves.

Mom and Astrid watched and laughed.

Then Apollo said, "People probably know Bruce Lee's name, but they might not know about his life or his work. I want to learn more about him and teach people about the things he accomplished."

"That's terrific, Apollo," Mom said. "That makes me wonder . . .

Astrid, what if you pick someone that *not* everyone is familiar with? Someone who did something fantastic, but that people might not know about."

Astrid's eyes lit up. "I like that idea."

Dad nodded. "That way, you could teach others about a new person who was important in history. At the same time, you could learn about someone you didn't know about before."

Astrid nodded too. "I *love* that idea! Teach others *and* myself about a new person so we can all discover an unknown hero!"

Suddenly, a book flew into the room and landed by Astrid's feet.

It was the picture book she had tripped over before—the one with the Asian woman on the cover.

Astrid picked it up and set it on the coffee table. "What is this?"

"That's Eliana's favorite new book," said Mom.

"Gao Chee, stop throwing books," Dad said as another book came crashing in from the hallway. "Now!"

"Sowwy!" Eliana yelled from the hall. She peeked her head around the corner and made her sorry face. Then she saw the book on the coffee table and said, "Nia Thy!"

Astrid and Apollo laughed.

"She thinks this woman looks like Grandma?" asked Astrid.

Mom nodded. "That's why she wanted to get it from the library. She said Grandma's on the cover," Mom explained with a laugh.

"Speaking of the library, tomorrow's media center day, Astrid," Apollo said. "You could ask Ms. Ahmed to help you research. Librarians are good at that."

"Thanks. I will!" said Astrid.

Now she was excited. She would pick someone who had made a mark in history that more people should know about.

Eliana ran into the room wearing her toy crown and carrying her toy shield again. "Weed Nia Thy to me!" she demanded and put her book on Astrid's lap.

"Maybe later, Eliana," Astrid said. "I've got some thinking to do." She handed the book back to her sister and patted her on the head.

* * *

The next day, Astrid and Apollo's class visited the media center. The media specialist talked to them about finding biographies for the Wax Museum project. She explained that biographies were about important people. Then the students began looking for books.

Astrid went up to her. "Hi, Ms. Ahmed," she said. "Can you please help me?"

"Sure," Ms. Ahmed replied. "Who have you decided to research?"

"That's the part I need help with. I can't decide," said Astrid.

Ms. Ahmed smiled and said, "Come this way." She took Astrid to a shelf under a window that faced the hallway. The shelf was labeled *Biographies.*

"Do you know what field of work you want to focus on?" Ms. Ahmed asked.

Astrid saw books about astronauts, inventors, teachers, and artists. "I'm not sure yet," she said. "I only know I want to pick a woman, someone who faced difficulties and still went on to do wonderful things."

Ms. Ahmed ran her finger along the spines of books and pulled out a few. She handed the books to Astrid.

"Here are biographies about women who made big contributions to the world."

"Thank you!" said Astrid.

She looked up to see her science teacher walking past the window. She remembered Mrs. Jackson talking about physics the day before.

Astrid suddenly had an idea. "I want to do my project on a scientist!"

"Great minds think alike!" said Ms. Ahmed and laughed. "It just so happens that all these books are about female scientists."

CHAPTER 4

Perfect Costume

"Stick your arms straight out," Mom said.

Apollo stretched out his arms. Mom placed a measuring tape from his shoulder to his wrist.

"Done with the sleeves. Now for your pants," she said. She measured from his waist to his ankles.

Astrid, Eliana, and Luna sat on the couch and watched them. Apollo was lucky!

Mom was already starting to make his Bruce Lee costume.

Astrid knew it would be perfect. Meanwhile, she hadn't even picked a person for her project yet.

Astrid turned back to look at the books she had checked out from the media center. She was happy she had decided to pick a woman scientist. Now she just had to choose the person. It was hard to decide!

One book was about Marie Curie, who discovered radioactivity and helped find treatments for cancer.

The next book was about a NASA mathematician named Katherine Johnson. She found a way for spacecraft to travel around Earth and to the moon.

There were other biographies too.

But Astrid had heard all the names of the scientists in these biographies before. Mrs. Jackson talked about these women in science class during Women's History Month.

Astrid wanted to research someone whose name people might not know.

Mom stood up and patted Apollo's shoulder. "I'm done measuring now. I have some yellow fabric I can use for this costume. Astrid, have you decided who you'll research?" she asked.

"Not yet," said Astrid, shaking her head.

Mom nodded. "Okay, I'll get started on Apollo's costume, while you keep thinking."

"Thanks, Mom!" Apollo called as Mom walked out of the room with her measuring tape.

Eliana jumped off the couch. She picked up a picture book and pretended to read to Luna.

"Luna, listen! Luna, look!" Eliana said as she tried to show the pictures to the dog.

Luna laid her head on the floor and closed her eyes.

Eliana kept pretend-reading. "One day, la-la-la and then the 'nother day, la-la-la . . ."

Apollo plopped down next to Astrid. He opened his book about Bruce Lee.

"I'm learning a lot from this book!

Did you know Bruce Lee was born in California? When he was young, he was a really good fighter *and* a good dancer," he said.

Astrid smiled. "What else?"

"When he got older, he taught kung fu to friends first. Then he opened a kung fu school. Later, he played Kato on *The Green Hornet* show on TV," said Apollo.

"I've heard of that show. It's about a superhero, right? It's super old!" said Astrid.

"Yeah! Then he started acting in movies and he got more famous. He wrote a book about his kung fu style called Jeet Kune Do," said Apollo.

"I want to read that!" said Astrid.

"Bruce Lee is famous for being a kung fu expert and movie star, but another thing I learned is that he really cared about how Asian people were shown in American movies. That's the thing I like most about him," said Apollo.

"That's important," Astrid said.

Apollo nodded. "I'm glad I picked Bruce Lee! Not only because he's Asian like me, but because he was really smart."

Astrid liked that about Bruce Lee too. She looked at her library books. She wished she had a book about a scientist who was Asian.

"Did you get good books from the media center?" Apollo asked.

He looked at the pile in her lap.

"I did. These are all about women scientists. But I wish there was one about an Asian woman scientist," she said.

Eliana closed her book and stood up. "Pway time!" she yelled. Luna's eyes popped open as Eliana grabbed her toy sword and adjusted the crown on her head.

"Are you a queen or a knight?" Apollo teased her.

"BOFE!" Eliana answered and pointed the toy sword into the air.

Suddenly, Astrid remembered Eliana's favorite picture book, the one with the Asian woman on the cover. Luna was now sitting on top of it.

"Can I see that, Eliana?" Astrid asked, pointing.

Eliana nodded and said, "Scooz me, Luna." But Luna didn't move. Eliana pulled the book out from under Luna, startling the dog. Luna trotted off to the kitchen.

Eliana handed it to Astrid and said, "Nia Thy!"

Astrid smiled. She read the title and looked at the cover more carefully. This wasn't about their grandmother, but it was about a physicist! Her name was Chien-Shiung Wu. She was the first woman to become president of the American Physical Society, a group of scientists who studied physics.

Apollo looked at the book too.

"Hey, we learned about physics the other day!" he said.

"I know," said Astrid. "This scientist did amazing work, but I've never heard her name. Have you?"

Apollo shook his head and read the back cover. "She worked on a secret project during World War II. She made important discoveries in physics. Everyone should know about her!"

Astrid opened the book and looked inside. She learned that Chien-Shiung Wu had performed special experiments, but she didn't always get credit for her work because she was a woman.

"The book says she had a lot of nicknames, like 'Madame Wu' and 'First Lady of Physics' and 'Queen of Nuclear Research,'" Astrid said.

"QWEEN!" Eliana shouted and posed in her crown.

Astrid and Apollo laughed.

When Astrid was done reading, she knew who to be for the wax museum. Someone who had faced challenges in life and worked hard. Someone who had done extraordinary things. Someone whose name not many people knew.

She would be Chien-Shiung Wu, the Queen of Nuclear Research and First Lady of Physics.

CHAPTER 5

Physics Queen

It was the day of the Living Wax Museum. The school hallway hummed with the sound of excited students. Some were already dressed in their costumes.

Apollo took off his jacket, revealing his yellow and black jumpsuit underneath.

Astrid hung her jacket on the coat hook. From her backpack, she pulled out the white lab coat that Mom made her. She slipped it on over her top and said, "Let's go!"

She and Apollo walked into the room. Right away, Astrid noticed it. All around the room, other students were wearing white lab coats too.

"White lab coats everywhere!" Apollo said.

"I guess so!" said Astrid in surprise.

Kiran was wearing a lab coat too. He came over and said, "Hi, I'm Albert Einstein. I developed the theory of relativity." Kiran's hair was messy with white flour sprinkled in it. It was sticking out in all directions to look like Einstein's poofy gray hair.

Next Lily came up to them in a white lab coat. "Hi, I'm Clara Barton. I'm a nurse who founded the Red Cross."

Sabina walked by. She had a white lab coat too!

"Are you a scientist or nurse?" Apollo asked her.

Sabina shook her head. "I'm Virginia Apgar. I'm a doctor who invented the Apgar score, which is a way to measure the health of newborn babies."

Sabina turned to Astrid. "Are you a scientist?"

Astrid thought it was great that so many students had chosen women in science fields! But she was pretty sure she was the only Chien-Shiung Wu in the room, and she was proud.

"I am Chien-Shiung Wu, a physicist," Astrid announced.

Lily, Sabina, and Kiran nodded and listened to her.

"I'm the first woman to be the president of the American Physical Society. I did research on uranium metal. I made many important discoveries. I even worked on a top-secret project! I hope after today, more people will know about me," said Astrid.

"That's nice! I've never heard your name before," said Lily.

"Neither have I," said Sabina. "Thanks for telling us about her work—or *your* work." Sabina and Astrid both giggled.

"Yes, thank you, Astrid! I mean Chien-Shiung Wu," Kiran said.

"Nice to meet you!" He shook Astrid's hand like a grown-up.

Astrid smiled. "You're welcome! I also have nicknames, like 'Queen of Nuclear Research.'"

"Well, thank you, Queen!" Kiran said and then he bowed before Astrid, making everyone laugh.

Astrid felt better, even if she and many of her friends were all wearing white lab coats.

She pointed at Apollo. "And this is Bruce Lee!"

Their friends turned to Apollo.

Apollo did a couple martial arts moves. The other kids clapped and ooh'd and ahh'd at his cool kung fu skills.

Apollo said, "Actually, most of you may know me, Bruce Lee, as the greatest kung fu movie star. But I also did other things. I taught people about martial arts and about Chinese culture. I worked hard to make sure Asian people were shown in positive ways in movies."

"Cool! I want to hear more about you too! My dad and I love your movies!" said Kiran.

Astrid and Apollo smiled at each other. They were proud of their wax museum choices.

Mrs. Lor came up to them. "You all look spectacular! This will be a wonderful wax museum," she said.

"Now, let's push our desks out of the way so visitors have room to walk around. Don't forget your buttons!"

Each student had a little button in front of them for visitors to press to learn about them. When a student's button was pushed, the student would come to life and tell about their accomplishments.

They heard voices in the hall. The visitors were here! The students rushed to their spots and then froze into their positions.

The visitors entered the room. Family members and students from other classes walked among the wax figures. The wax figures tried hard not to laugh!

The twins spotted their parents and Eliana. Eliana was wearing her toy crown, as usual. Mom and Dad smiled at them. The twins tried not to smile back because statues didn't smile.

"Remember not to speak until a visitor pushes on your button," Mrs. Lor whispered.

The students nodded, then quickly held still again. Statues didn't nod either!

Their science teacher, Mrs. Jackson, walked in. She came right up to Astrid and pressed her button.

"Hello," said Astrid. "I am Chien-Shiung Wu. I am a physicist known as the 'Queen of Nuclear Research.'"

Mrs. Jackson burst into a smile and said, "Wonderful!"

Astrid told her about Chien-Shiung Wu's life. She talked about how, when she was a little girl in China, people didn't really want girls to go to school. When she was an adult in America, she didn't win science awards because she was a woman—even though she did the work. Astrid told other interesting facts about her life as well.

When Astrid was done speaking, Mrs. Jackson said, "Excellent work!" She gave Astrid a quiet round of applause.

Then Astrid noticed Eliana shyly staring at the other students.

Eliana walked over and stared at Astrid next. She had a puzzled look on her face.

Eliana turned to Mom and Dad and pulled on their shirts. She said, "Why same?"

Mom looked at the students. She looked at Astrid.

Then Dad said, "They're scientists or doctors or nurses. They may have the same uniform, but each student is a different person."

Eliana thought about it. Then her eyes grew big. She took off her crown and reached up on her tippy-toes to place it on Astrid's head.

"QWEEN!" Eliana said, delighted. Astrid couldn't help but smile.

"Thank you!" Astrid said to her sister, even though she wasn't supposed to talk yet. She couldn't help it. Eliana had made her costume perfect, just like Apollo's!

"Push my button!" Astrid whispered.

Eliana eagerly pushed the button.

Astrid, the 'Queen of Physics,' came to life and proudly told her family about the amazing life of Chien-Shiung Wu.

- Hmong people first lived in southern China. Many of them moved to Southeast Asia in the 1800s. Some Hmong decided to stay in the country of Laos (pronounced *LAH-ohs*).

LAOS

- In the 1950s, a war called the Vietnam War started in Southeast Asia. The United States joined this war. They asked the Hmong in Laos to help them. When the U.S. lost the war, Hmong people had to leave Laos.

- After 1975, many Hmong came to the U.S. as refugees. Refugees are people who escape from their country to find a new, safe place to live. Today, Minnesota is home to around 80,000 Hmong.

- Many Hmong American families enjoy outdoor activities like camping, boating, and fishing.

Does your class or school do a wax museum project? If not, plan one with your friends!

First, make a list of famous people you admire. Then ask yourself why they are important to you. You might have to do some research to answer that question! Decide who feels like the best choice to you.

Next, find out as much as you can about the person you chose. Here are some questions to answer:

- When and where was I born?
- Do I have brothers and sisters?
- What did I like best in school?
- Did I go to college?
- What am I famous for?
- What is my biggest accomplishment?
- Why should people know more about me?

Finally, make a costume and maybe some props! If you chose a scientist, you can make a pretend microscope out of cardboard tubes. If you chose an athlete, put on your sneakers and copy your hero's style! You might find lots of options in your closets at home—just be sure to ask your family members first. Then, invite them to your wax museum!

accomplish (ah-KAHMP-lish)—to succeed in finishing something or doing something well

biography (by-OGG-graf-ee)—information about a person written by someone else

contribution (kahn-trih-BYU-shun)—the giving of something that plays a big part in making something happen

historical (his-TORR-uh-kuhl)—from history or having to do with history

martial arts (MAR-shul ARTS)—specific types of fighting or self-defense styles that are popular as sports

nuclear (NEW-klee-ur)—having to do with the energy created by splitting atoms

physics (FIZZ-iks)—a science that deals with matter and energy and how they interact

radioactivity (ray-dee-oh-ak-TIV-uh-tee)—a process in which atoms break apart and create a lot of energy

theory (THEER-ee)—an idea accepted by science that explains something

uranium (yur-RAY-nee-um)—a metallic element that is radioactive

1. Astrid feels that it's important to choose a female Asian scientist for her research project. Why do you think this is important to her? Why is it especially important for women and people of color to have their stories told?

2. If you could choose anyone for a wax museum project, who would you choose? Why?

3. Biographies in the media center or library are a great way to learn things about important people. Besides books, what are some other ways you can find information?

4. Many famous people, such as Amelia Earhart, are listed in this story as options for the research project. How many famous names can you find in the story? Make a list. Would you choose any of these people to research?

5. Apollo chose Bruce Lee for his wax museum project. What are three reasons Apollo chose him? Write them down.

6. Students are often asked to do research on famous people. But many important people aren't famous at all. Write a paragraph about someone in your family or community who is important to you, and explain why they are important.

ABOUT THE AUTHOR

V.T. Bidania has been writing stories ever since she was five years old. She was born in Laos and grew up in St. Paul, Minnesota, right where Astrid and Apollo live! She has an MFA in creative writing from The New School and is a McKnight Writing Fellow. She lives outside of the Twin Cities and spends her free time reading all the books she can find, writing more stories, and playing with her family's sweet Morkie.

ABOUT THE ILLUSTRATOR

César Samaniego was born in Barcelona. He grew up with an artist father, smelling his father's oils, reading his comic books, and trying to paint over his father's illustrations! He attended Llotja Arts and Crafts School and graduated with honors in 2010. Since then César has published many books and provided art for apps, textbooks, and animations. He lives in Canet de Mar, a small town on the coast of Barcelona, with his wife, daughter, five cats, and a crazy dog.